W9-DIZ-550

MY FIRST LOOK AT COUNTRIES

**A CITY IN CHINA AT NIGHT**

# China

ADELE RICHARDSON

CREATIVE EDUCATION

Published by Creative Education

123 South Broad Street, Mankato, Minnesota 56001

Creative Education is an imprint of The Creative Company

Designed by Rita Marshall

Photographs by Getty Images (Barry C. Bishop, Cancan Chu, D E Cox, Garry Hunter,

Gareth Jones, John Lamb, Yann Layma, Keren Su)

Copyright © 2007 Creative Education

Printed in the United States of America

**Library of Congress Cataloging-in-Publication Data**

Richardson, Adele. China / by Adele Richardson.

p. cm. — (My first look at countries)

Includes index.

ISBN-13 : 978-1-58341-445-3

1. China—Juvenile literature. I. Title. II. Series.

DS706.R48 2005          951—dc22          2005051052

First edition  9 8 7 6 5 4 3 2 1

# CHINA

## A Big Country

China is a country on Earth's biggest **continent**. The continent is called Asia. China is on the east side of Asia. East is the right side of Asia on a map.

China is a big country. It is the third biggest country in the world! Only Russia and Canada are bigger.

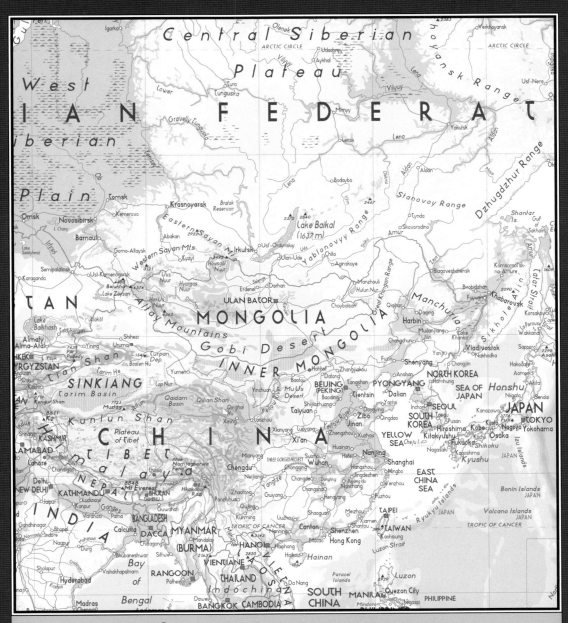

CHINA LOOKS BIG ON MAPS AND GLOBES

China has all kinds of weather. The south, or bottom, part of China gets very hot in the summer. It is not cold for long in the winter there. But the north, or top, part of China gets very cold in the winter. Some parts of China get lots of rain. Other parts are dry.

China touches Mount
Everest. It is the tallest
mountain in the world.

## The Land, the Wall

Most people in China live on the east, or right, side. Most big cities in China are on the east side. Some farms are there, too. There is good soil for growing food on the east side of China.

**Desert** covers the west side of China. West is the left side of China on a map. China has big mountains, too. The world's highest

School kids in China

exercise 10 minutes every

morning before class starts.

KIDS EXERCISING ON THEIR SCHOOL'S ROOF

**plateau** (*plah-TOW*) is in China. It is called the Tibet Plateau.

In the north part of China is a big wall. It is called the Great Wall of China. It is longer than the United States. The Great Wall of China was built a long time ago.

**PART OF THE GREAT WALL OF CHINA**

## China's Animals

Many kinds of animals live in China. Deer and goats live in China. So do alligators. Lots of birds live in China, too. Colorful peacocks and orioles live there.

Some of China's animals are **endangered**. Tigers and snow leopards are endangered. So are river dolphins. Some people in China work to keep endangered animals safe.

**THERE ARE NOT MANY TIGERS LEFT IN CHINA**

China's most famous animal is the giant panda. Giant pandas look like big black and white bears. They only eat a plant called bamboo. Giant pandas are endangered. There are not many of them left in the world.

## Lots of People

China has more people than any other country. More than a billion people live there! Most people in China live in cities. Others live in small towns in the country.

China's writing is one
of the oldest kinds of
writing in the world.

SOME PEOPLE IN CHINA WORK IN RICE FIELDS

The main language in China is called Mandarin. But not all people in China speak Mandarin. There are more than 12 languages in China!

Most people in China eat lots of rice. Sometimes they make the rice into a hot cereal for breakfast. Other times, they fry it in a pan with **vegetables**. People in China drink lots of tea, too. People all over the world like China's food and tea!

**EATING WITH LONG STICKS CALLED CHOPSTICKS**

# Hands-on: Panda Face

Giant pandas are endangered. But you can see one every day by making a giant panda face!

## What You Need

Two paper plates

A black crayon

Tape

Scissors

## What You Do

1. Ask a grown-up to help you cut out two circles from one paper plate. The circles should be the size of a tennis ball. Color them black.
2. Tape the circles to the back of the other plate. They should stick up at the top like ears.
3. On the front of the plate, draw eyes, a nose, and a mouth. Enjoy your panda face!

A GIANT PANDA EATING BAMBOO

## Index

## Words to Know

**continent**—one of Earth's seven big pieces of land

**desert**—a dry, sandy area where few plants and trees grow

**endangered**—an animal that might die out so that there are no more left on Earth

**plateau**—an area of high, flat land

**vegetables**—plants that can be eaten; lettuce, broccoli, and celery are all vegetables

## Read More

Fontes, Justine and Ron. *China.* New York: Children's Press, 2004.

Roza, Greg. *A Primary Source Guide to China.* New York: PowerKids Press, 2003.

Schroeder, Holly. *China ABCs: A Book About the People and Places of China.*
    Minneapolis: Picture Window Books, 2004.

## Explore the Web

**ABCs of China** http://www.fi.edu/fellows/fellow1/apr99/abc

**Ask Asia** http://www.askasia.org/students/virtual_gallery/student_art_showcase/
    stud_art_show.htm

**Enchanted Learning: All About China** http://www.enchantedlearning.com/
    asia/China